JOSEPH SMITH'S ELEVEN-DOLLAR SURGERY

Joseph Smith's Eleven-Dollar Surgery

Blaine and Brenton Yorgason

GRANDIN BOOK COMPANY

OREM, UTAH

ISBN 0-910523-44-4

Preface

WE WROTE THIS BOOK primarily to instruct and edify our own families. As young men we had very little knowledge of the details of the early life of Joseph Smith Jr.; so with this story we are doing our best to see that our children, and perhaps their children, will come to know and appreciate the early experiences of the first prophet of this dispensation.

Hopefully, we can show that, from the earliest recorded events, the life of Joseph Smith Jr. was in the Lord's hands and that the Prophet was preserved, protected, and tutored by him.

Dr. LeRoy S. Wirthlin, formerly an assistant professor of surgery at Harvard Medical School and currently a vascular surgeon in Detroit, Michigan, wrote:

> For members of The Church of Jesus Christ of Latter-day Saints it is important to realize that Joseph Smith received treatment that was generations ahead of current practice and was attended to, on at least one occasion, by the most highly trained and experienced physician in Northern New England who was

also the only physician in the Untied States who aggressively and successfully operated for osteomyelitis and thereby prevented amputation. Thus Joseph received the best of care that was available from a giant of a man who lived, taught, and practiced in Hanover, New Hampshire, only a few miles from Joseph's home.

Finally, knowing how learning of these early events has benefited our own testimonies, we hope that sharing what has been recorded and adding a fairly heavy touch of color and detail, will spark in others a similar kinship with and appreciation for Joseph Smith, the Prophet.

Introduction

THE FOLLOWING ACCOUNT is most properly termed historical fiction. Joseph Smith Jr. wrote only one, less complete document that resembles it. Appendix A contains that document in its entirety.

Although much of the detail of the events described herein is speculative, based on Joseph's account and the records of others, we do know a great deal of that particular experience. In fact, it is the Smiths' only experience, prior to the First Vision, that is recorded in detail.

Joseph once said he had learned many lessons from this sickness. He likely grew closer to Hyrum and to his father at this time, for they were particularly attentive to Joseph as our account describes. These relationships were to prove crucial in the years ahead, and it seems to us that the Lord allowed this disease to strengthen their feelings for each other.

Joseph apparently also learned how much pain he could endure, and that too came in handy later in his life. He learned, as well, how to respond to the criticism of his playmates, who teased and taunted him because of his limp. Overcoming childish criticism obviously helped him to deal with later persecutions.

Perhaps, however, the greatest lesson Joseph and his family learned from his illness and subsequent recovery was that Heavenly Father loved them. If Joseph did not receive a testimony of prayer when Sophronia's life was given back to her, then he had to have received such after his own life was spared. Therefore it seems likely that this experience helped give him the confidence in the spring of 1820 to learn from the scriptures and ultimately inquire openly of the Lord.

Chapter I

"ELEVEN DOLLARS?"

My father's words were almost a whisper as he repeated Doctor Nathan Smith's fee.[1] "Eleven whole dollars?"

The question hung in the early afternoon air. The room was hot and muggy and filled with people, all of them looking as uncomfortable as I felt.

I watched them from where I lay on the table. I was sprawled out helpless and waiting, bathed in sweat, my skin sticking to the rough-hewn boards. For what seemed like a long time after my father's question, the room was silent—silent, except for the buzzing of bottle-flies.

At last, taking a deep breath, Father spoke again. "Sir," he said honestly to the gray-haired doctor, "I simply do not have that much money."

Doctor Smith's expression did not change. His eyes, which I thought were kindly, went from Father to Mother and there hesitated as he gazed upon her grieving face. His eyes then shifted around our small, rented home,[2] which was sparsely furnished but clean. He finally focused on me.

Sprawled out as I was on the table, with my swollen and infected leg bare to my hip, I must have been a miserable sight. Still, I did my best to smile in response to the doctor's compassionate gaze.

"Are you all right, boy?" the doctor asked gently.

"Yes sir," I answered gamely. Actually I was struggling with the heat, my head hurt where it lay against the boards, the old sore under my arm was acting up again, and my leg ached like the very devil himself was inside it. The open wound smelled bad too, but I had grown used to that and hardly noticed it anymore.

Outside a horse nickered, another stomped its hoof, and for perhaps the hundredth time I looked up at the faces of the dozen or so people, most of whom were visitors, who stood around the table. It was their horses that I could hear stomping and nickering outside; it was the expressions on their faces that by then had me petrified with fear.

I felt afraid with everyone paying attention to me. But what scared me most of all were the fearful and concerned expressions on my parents' faces. They were more than worried, and I could sense it.

"Mr. and Mrs. Smith," Doctor Smith finally spoke, "your son is in a bad way, and we must act immediately. I think the money should be the last of your concerns."

"Are you saying that you expect him to die?" Father asked.

"Joseph," Mother scolded, "of course he won't die. Where in the name of heaven is your faith?"

I gulped a little, wincing in pain, and looked again at the serious faces of the men who surrounded me. Clearly they felt I was going to die—I had no doubt of that.

Looking past them, I could see my older brothers, Alvin and Hyrum, and back in the corner, Sophronia, my older sister. None of them were smiling either, and if I hadn't hurt so bad or felt so terrified, I might have laughed. They looked like they were going to a funeral.

However, as I thought it through, I realized that in spite of the fear in the room, I felt as my mother did. I knew I wasn't going to die. After all, Sophronia had had her miracle, and I could sure tough this out until the good Lord gave me mine.

"What do you recommend, Doctor Smith?" Mother asked then. "What must we do to save the boy's life?"[3]

Doctor Perkins coughed, Doctor Stone turned away, but Doctor Smith, who seemed a little older, was not one to hide his thoughts or to beat around the bush.

"If I'd been asked to come three weeks ago, ma'am, I might have saved his life and his leg both. Now, however, it may be too late. As you know, he has lost a great deal of blood and strength in these last few weeks. Because of this, I fear what the consequences would be should we even try to operate."[4]

The hush that filled the room was so loud I could hear my heart beating. It was loud inside my head, steady, hammering.

Lose my leg? my mind cried out in silent anguish. Oh, no! That can't happen! It just can't! Dear God above, don't let me lose my leg! I know you won't let me lose my leg.

How on earth, I wondered as tears clouded my eyes, would I ever be able to get around? I only knew one man who had lost a leg—Peg-leg Rawlins,[5] I think his name was—and though he was game as could be, there was a great deal that he could not do.

Besides that, how would I ever become a soldier like my Grandfather Asael or my Great-grandfather Samuel?[6] They had both served in the war of the Revolution; and with the war with England now in progress, the prospects seemed good that I might one day become a soldier too.

But not with one leg I wouldn't! No, sir, not with one leg.

Chapter II

So THAT SUMMER IN 1813[1] I lay on my family's table confidently expecting my miracle. I was seven years old at the time, almost halfway to eight, and for one of such an age, miracles hardly seemed miraculous at all.

Now I am a little older, and Mother feels that I can look back and put it in perspective. So I am writing of my miracle, hoping that I can tell it right and leave nothing out that would be important.

Our family lived in Lebanon, New Hampshire, and I held the middle position in the family. Two brothers and a sister were older, and two brothers and a sister were younger.

The rented cabin where we lived that year was small—two rooms and a loft. But it was snug and warm in the winter and not too difficult to keep clean. Like all large families in small homes, however, we seemed always to be getting in each other's way. Still, Father reminded us frequently that we were fortunate to have a tight roof over our heads. That was Father, always looking for the good in things. We children liked that about him, and most of my brothers and sisters picked up the same characteristic. I'm trying to be that way myself.

My oldest brother's name is Alvin, and the year of my surgery he was thirteen years old.[2] Father called him a man, and even though he was always getting into some sort of mischief, Father depended on him. To us young ones, Alvin seemed uncommonly smart, and he constantly did little things to teach us without our knowing we were being taught. He wanted us to grow up right, and he was bound that if it were left up to him, we would. Alvin seemed especially concerned about me and was always teaching, correcting, and encouraging me in his own quiet way to do better than I had done before.

Next to Alvin is Hyrum,[3] who is four years older than I am and who was eleven that summer of 1813. Hyrum and I have always been close, and that closeness began with my surgery.

Mother and Father named their eldest daughter Sophronia,[4] though the youngsters and I call her Sophie. She is two years older than me and frequently plays mother to the rest of us, which Mother tells me is almost always the case with older sisters. Some days she seems mighty bossy. But as we get older we grow closer, and I am not so troubled by it. That summer Sophronia carried much of the burden of keeping the home going so Mother could devote her time to caring for me.

Besides those three, I have two younger brothers and a baby sister. The baby we call Catherine,[5] and she was born July 28, the year before my surgery. My younger brothers start with Samuel,[6] who was five years old when my leg got so bad. He was born on

March 13, which began a string of rather unusual events for our family. On the day Samuel turned two, which was three years before my illness, Mother had another baby boy. She and Father both liked names from the Bible so they named him Ephraim.[7] I was only four years old at the time, but I remember being excited that I had two brothers with the same birthday.

Ephraim wasn't well, however, and though we did all we could for him, it wasn't enough. He died early in the morning of his eleventh day of life. The entire family grieved, but Mother took his death the hardest and didn't get over her loneliness for baby Ephraim until exactly one year later.

Mother's grief ended on March 13, when she gave birth to a third baby boy. We all gathered together that time and, instead of picking a name from the Bible, decided to call him William.[8] And so William he became.

But the unusual circumstance of having the last three sons born on the same day, the thirteenth day of March, has always been a source of pride and not a little wonderment to all of us.

As far as the Smith family is concerned, I've said about all there is to say except that we all got ill that summer, and not one of us felt much like doing anything—especially me, for I was in terrible pain, and I thought it was never going to go away.

Chapter III

"Mother," Father declared quietly, while the children and I strained to hear, "I'm stumped. At last count there was less than two dollars in the crock, and I have no notion where any more will come from. I've racked my brain, and I can think of no quick way to earn enough cash to pay Doctor Smith."

Mother reached out and put her hand across my father's hand. "But Joseph," she declared firmly, "the boy needs help, and the good Lord knows it. I'm sure he will provide."

"I know that, Lucy. But the Lord isn't here, or at least he hasn't come forward with any money the last day or so. And no self-respecting man can ask another to give free service. Leastwise, no Smith can!"

"Mr. Smith," the doctor interrupted, "I don't think—"

"Doctor," Mother cut him off sharply, suddenly smiling with an idea, "does your family need poultry?"[1]

Doctor Smith grinned in return, "Poultry, ma'am? I've growing sons and daughters, and I've recently accepted a position down in New Haven, Connecticut, at Yale University. I would hope to provide food for my family while I am gone, and poultry would be a great help."[2]

Mother beamed, and I was somewhat relieved myself; for knowing her, I knew where this conversation was heading.

"Then it is settled," she said, smiling. "Alvin, would you and Hyrum gather a dozen hens and one rooster and pen them for the good doctor?"

"Right now, Mother?" Hyrum asked, sounding terribly disappointed. "But can't we stay until. . ."

Suddenly embarrassed, Hyrum looked from Mother to me, and then slowly dropped his gaze to the floor.

"Come, Hyrum," Alvin declared quickly, taking Hyrum by the shoulder. "We'd best be getting busy."

Reluctantly Hyrum followed Alvin out the door, and as they headed for the chicken yard the sound of their arguing voices drifted back to us. Hyrum was saying it was a foolish idea to give away so many chickens just so my leg could get cut off, and Alvin was arguing that the Lord had given our family those hens and rooster so there would be an honorable way to pay for my surgery and that I wasn't going to lose my leg anyway.

I agreed with Alvin and was relieved to note that by the time my two brothers were out of earshot, he had convinced Hyrum as well.

Absently Mother shooed away a swarm of bottle-flies which had once again settled around my leg. I'd heard of some doctors using flies and maggots to clean wounds,[3] but to my way of thinking it was a mighty poor idea. I certainly didn't want such a practice tried on me.

Of course, maybe it wouldn't matter anyway. Nothing else had helped much, and as I gazed at the ugly, open wound on my leg, I could hardly imagine what had happened to me.

When she looked up from shooing the flies away, Mother's eyes were filled with tears. Her crying bothered me, for when she cried it was all I could do to keep myself from tearing up. Not that I felt sorry for myself, although as I lay there in the hot room I had to admit that I did that too. But I didn't like to see my mother hurting, especially on account of me.

"Doctor Smith," Mother suddenly asked, brushing her eyes dry and ending the silence, "can you tell us about this disease that is attacking young Joseph?"

Doctor Perkins coughed again, and I could see that he was trying to catch my father's eye.

"Lucy," Father asked quietly after he had seen Doctor Perkins' signal. "Do you think it is a good idea for young Joseph to hear all of this?"

Mother looked down lovingly at me, and I looked back at her. Then because I didn't want to see her tears, I looked past her at the log beams in the ceiling, trying to focus on them and line them up with my eyes. That was one little way I had found to get my mind off my present circumstances. Soon I was concentrating so much on the beams and cross-timbers that I nearly forgot the almost unbearable pain in my leg.

The doctors who surrounded the table, however, hadn't forgotten at all. Most of them fidgeted somewhat and then were still—probably thankful that they didn't have to do any explaining. The host of flies buzzed about the room, and at last Mother answered Father's question.

"Joseph," she said as she took my hand, "your son is strong. With all he has endured[4] and what he is about to go through, he deserves to know what is happening. And I should think he would want to know."

Father nodded. "I believe you are right, my dear. I only wanted to make certain."

"Son?" he asked, turning to look down at me, "would you like to hear this, or would you rather we go outside and discuss it?"

"I would like to hear," I murmured, not certain whether I should or not. "The pain in my leg is tolerably bad anyway, and I can't see where a few words will make it hurt any worse."

Doctor Smith smiled warmly and began to explain my circumstances to all in the room.

"As you know," he said quietly, "the Connecticut River Valley is in the grip of a terrible epidemic of typhoid fever."[5]

"Typhoid?" Mother interrupted. "All the folks hereabouts are calling it typhus. Are they the same thing?"

"No. Typhoid and typhus are different diseases. Your son definitely has complications that arise from typhoid fever. In fact, I've not seen a single case of typhus in the district.

"So young Joseph had typhoid fever," he continued. "He partially recovered and now has developed this complication.[6]

Unfortunately, it is much more severe than my colleagues who previously treated him had imagined."

"And they did wrong?" Father asked. "In their treatment, I mean?"

"Sir," the doctor responded, "to declare that they did wrong would be a harsh judgment. Perhaps they knew no better. Yet the pain in his shoulder was what I call a soft-tissue abscess, not a sprained shoulder. Was he not treated for a sprain?"[7]

"He was," Mother stated. "We were told he had fallen and injured his shoulder in the fall."

"Exactly," Doctor Smith agreed. "Yet he hadn't fallen, and so of course the treatment didn't help. Soon the abscess developed under his arm, and the purulent material—pus—began to collect."

"That's so," I declared proudly, thankful that there was something in all of this that I could comprehend and respond to. "I saw Father and Doctor Parker press out an entire quart of fluid!"[8]

"I imagine they did," Doctor Smith replied as he placed his hand upon my perspiring forehead. "It's a wonder there wasn't more than what they obtained."

"We think," Doctor Perkins then stated, taking over the conversation from Doctor Smith, "that the disease travels in the blood down to the leg. How else it could get there we do not know; but because it has not been proven, we are forced to say that we only think it. However, once the disease is there in the long bones of the leg, it infects both the interior of the bone, or marrow, and the periosteum, the membrane surrounding the bone. New abscesses develop, and suppuration occurs."[9]

"Suppur. . . , " I stammered, trying to say the word. "What is suppur. . . ?"

"The dying of body tissue," Doctor Smith explained. "That is why there is so much purulent material draining from the wound in your leg. It is also why you lost that quart of infectious fluid from beneath your arm. Suppuration had occurred there as well."

"If my flesh is dead," I asked then, "why does it hurt so confounded much?"

"Of course it hurts, son," Doctor Smith responded. "The build-up of that purulent material causes pressure where the tissue is still alive, both inside and outside of the bone; and that is why you feel so much pain."

I nodded, though in truth I had no real idea of what either of the doctors were saying. Except for the pain, that is—I knew all about that!

"With the development of suppuration," Doctor Smith continued, "necrosis, or bone death, occurs. Look here, and I will show you."

Everyone gathered closer to look at my leg. I would have looked, but I was unable to lift myself into a sitting position. Still, I felt Doctor Smith probing inside my exposed leg, which caused my whole body to reel with pain.

I gasped as a section of tissue was pulled back. Tears filled my eyes, Mother took hold of my hand and held it tightly to her.

"Dear Joseph," she whispered through new tears of her own, "we do not mean to hurt you."

I knew that, I truly did. But it didn't seem to help. Everything hurt, and I felt it would never stop. Still, I took several deep breaths, closed my eyes tightly, and spoke through gritted teeth to my mother. "It's all right. The pain has passed, and I would like to hear the rest of it."

Mother squeezed my hand again and then nodded to the doctor.

"Do you see this discoloration?" Doctor Smith asked, pointing to a spot on my leg. "This is dead bone, called sequestrum. If left alone and if the boy lives that long, this dead bone will simply putrefy and create trouble. Meanwhile this mound of bone, which you see here on each end of the sequestrum is new bone, called involucrum. It will eventually envelope the dead bone. Thus the infection will remain locked in place and will always cause trouble."

"And the dead bone will never dissolve?" one of the young doctors asked.

"Not speedily," Doctor Smith responded. "However, portions of the bone will occasionally separate themselves from the living bone and work their way out through the new bone and flesh, where they may be plucked almost effortlessly out of the skin.[10] When that happens, it will cause a discharge that will likely persist for years. Amputation, of course, eliminates that problem and allows the patient to live a fairly normal life. That is why I wish for all of you to consider removing the boy's leg."

I swallowed, fearing the doctor's words more than I could express, for in my childish thoughts I had determined that I would rather die than lose my leg.

How had I come to that place, I wondered. How had I come to
the point where I might lose my leg? And where was God? He had
not answered my prayers for so many long agonizing days and
nights. Didn't he love me anymore? Didn't he hear me?

Mother and Father both said that he did, and I believed them.
Only, why hadn't my prayers been answered? It made no sense to
me, none at all.

Chapter IV

MY OWN ORDEAL STARTED LATE IN 1812, when Sophie was at her worst. Yet whereas my sister was down for ninety days, I was only in bed two weeks and felt that I had gotten off lucky.

While I was recovering, however, I awoke one morning with a dreadful pain in my left shoulder. When it started to swell, Mother put out word for Doctor Parker[1] to stop in the next time he was making his rounds in our district.

The doctor finally arrived and examined me but could see no sign of infection other than the swelling. He then mistakenly told Father and Mother that I had likely injured or sprained my shoulder in a fall. Of course I knew better, for I had been confined to my bed and home for over two weeks and had not fallen anywhere at all.

I informed Doctor Parker of that fact but was ignored. The doctor then applied some bone liniments and a hot shovel. And so my typhoid fever was treated as a sprain.

Of course the treatments didn't work. My shoulder continued to swell, and soon it was so bad that I could hardly stand the pain.

Concerned at the agony I suffered, Father and Mother got Doctor Parker back to the house as quickly as they could. After a brief examination the doctor realized he had made a mistake and quickly determined to lance the wound with his cutting knife.

I recollect being absolutely terrified at the thought of that knife slicing into my small body. But the doctor reaffirmed that such a procedure was the only way for me to regain my health.

Mother brought in a big pan, and carefully placed it under my shoulder. At that Alvin and Father took hold of me, and the doctor slit the sore open, almost before I knew what was happening.

After cutting open the fever blister, Dr. Parker squeezed and pressed; and if I had thought the cutting was bad, that squeezing and pressing almost did me in. By the time the doctor had finished, a full quart of what he called purulent matter had poured out into the pan.

I was sobbing by then and almost delirious with the pain.[2] Father held my head up throughout the procedure, or I probably would have fainted dead away. Despite the pain, I remained alert through the entire torture.

When he finished draining the blister, the doctor washed out the incision, told Mother to put hot poultices on the sore twice a day, and left me in my misery. I was so sore I could not stand to have anyone touch my shoulder. And no matter which way I lay, it would not cease. Still, twice a day like it was her religious duty, Mother fixed a hot poultice of linseed, bread, mustard, and oil,[3] spread it between two pieces of muslin, and applied it to my throbbing wound.

Truthfully I can't recollect if the hot poultice made things worse or better, but my mother persisted, and so, of course, I did also. The procedure of doctoring the wound lasted two weeks, and yet there was very little sign of change. Nor did I regain any of my strength.

Then one morning I was sitting in the kitchen with Father, both of us watching Mother while she made up a batch of bread. As I sat there a pain shot like lightning from my shoulder down into my left leg. In total agony I cried out, "Oh, Father! The pain is so severe, how can I bear it?"[4]

From that day my leg started to swell just as my shoulder had. For two weeks it continued to swell, while Mother spent almost every hour of the day and night carrying me around and trying to comfort me. Finally, totally exhausted, Mother went to bed, terribly ill herself and unable from that day to care for me.[5]

Hyrum then volunteered to care for me. I was placed upon a low bed, and Hyrum made himself as comfortable as possible next to me. He then took hold of my leg and squeezed it between his hands.[6]

Day and night for almost two weeks Hyrum did little else. For as long as he could without collapsing and then as quickly as he could get to it again, Hyrum held and squeezed my swollen and throbbing leg. Of course he had to stop occasionally, but whenever he did, the pain became so great that I would cry out and writhe with agony.

During that terribly difficult time, Hyrum became my only source of comfort.[7] Of course we visited a great deal during those two weeks, and we developed a strong familial bond. Hyrum told me stories of his adventures and exploits, and to my way of thinking, what he got into was little short of amazing. Laughter came hard to me that summer because of the pain, but Hyrum did his best to help me laugh and lift my spirits with his quiet humor.

Alvin helped, too, when he wasn't working with Father out in the fields. Through their laughter and love, they made that summer bearable.

After two weeks of Hyrum's dedicated care without seeing any improvement, Father sent for another doctor.[8] The doctor propped me up on the kitchen table, he stretched my leg out, and then while Father and Alvin held me down, he cut a slit from my knee to my ankle.[9]

I don't recall exactly how I behaved, but anyone would have cried out and done his best to twist away from the terrible agony, and I am certain I did all of that. Before the surgery that particular doctor told Father and Mother that by opening up my swollen leg, the infection would drain out immediately.[10] But only a small portion of the infection drained; and as the days went by and the wound closed, I felt worse than before.

Several days passed, and the pain became more violent than ever. I could hardly stand it. I was wasting away in body and spirit, and my incredible agony had such a debilitating effect upon my family that in desperation Father called the doctor a third time.

He came at once. I was held to the table, and the doctor operated once again. He squeezed and probed and enlarged the wound, doing his best to extract all the purulent material, and again I came close to passing out from the pain.

In these efforts to cleanse and empty the wound, the doctor cut even deeper, all the way to the bone. Satisfied, he left me weakened, exhausted, and near death. But my family hoped that at last things would turn around and I would recover.[11]

However, the infectious matter seemed to multiply faster than it could be removed, and again the surgery proved unsuccessful. My leg continued to increase in size, while at the same time the rest of my body dwindled away.[12]

At last Father called a family council. Apparently he had heard of a good surgeon, who might know how to cure me of my illness. After much discussion, Father sent for this surgeon.

Doctor Nathan Smith proved equal to his reputation. From what I have been told, Doctor Smith had established the medical school at the new Dartmouth College, located only five miles from our home. He had intended to have already moved down to Yale. But he later said that the typhoid epidemic had become so deadly that he had feared to leave his family in such peril and so had remained.[13] And his fears had not been groundless; that year four of his children were affected by typhoid fever.[14]

The epidemic was so widespread that according to Doctor Smith, in one town in our vicinity, the citizens had buried over fifty persons since the first of that year of 1813.[15]

From all that Mother and Father learned, Doctor Smith was one of the two most able bone doctors in the world, and the only surgeon in our entire United States who had a ghost of a chance of saving my life and my leg. And there he was within five miles of our home. It was as though he had been placed and kept there by the Lord just to take care of me.[16]

Sophie's miracle had taught me well, and so for days I had silently prayed that someone would come who would know what to do. Therefore I wasn't surprised when Father located Doctor Nathan Smith.

When the doctor arrived at our home, he brought his partner, Cyrus Perkin, a third man named Doctor Stone, and several young medical students.

Ten or eleven men crowded into our small home.[17] At first they met with my parents and briefly discussed what I had been through and what my possibilities were. From there they all crowded to my bedside.

When all were in the room, Doctor Smith spoke directly to me.

"My poor boy, we have come to take care of you."

"Yes," I answered, "I see you have. But you have not come to take my leg, have you, sir?"[18]

Though they didn't answer me, in my heart I knew that most all of them expected that I would either die or lose my leg.[19] Somehow, though, I felt certain that I would not die, and I was not about to let them take my leg.

For some time the doctors examined my leg and discussed it, and the entire family anxiously waited their decision.

I was terrified. They were discussing amputation, and I didn't want to hear of it. I could not bear the thought of losing my leg. I wanted to keep it for all the things I wanted to do in my life.[20]

There was something else I was thinking of, too. Over and over I thought of the morning when Mother and Father prayed for Sophie. And I had seen her miracle. I prayed and hoped that could happen for me as well.

And that hope, according to Mother, is the beginning of faith.

Chapter V

Typhoid is a dreadful disease. Everyone fears it, no one knows what causes it, and no cure has been found other than faith.[1] Mother has a great deal of faith, and Father does too, even though he is not active in any church. The remainder of us—though I'm certain we all believe—have uncertain quantities of faith.

But to get on. Father said we could tell who contracted typhoid because their body would waste away in fever. Then they would get dizzy out of their head and finally become unconscious. Once this happened, their skin would change color, their tongue would turn black, and shortly after that they would die.[2]

Well, our family was victimized with this plague. Each of the children was stricken by it, but Sophie was hit the hardest. As Alvin, Hyrum, and I thought back on it, she was sick for over ninety days.[3] Mother kept track on the day-and-date calendar she had on the wall; and to make certain of my record, I dug it out of her trunk and checked.

Actually all us children were moping around the house, still sick, when Sophie's miracle took place. It began on the eighty-ninth day of her illness, when her pupils suddenly dilated, and she slipped into a deathlike sleep.[4]

When this happened, Mother quickly ran and fetched a midwife to come over to our house to help her bathe Sophie's body. Both of them continued to bathe Sophie through the night.

Except for Father, the rest of us went to bed, too sick ourselves to think much about Sophie. I don't intend to imply that we weren't worried about her, because we were. It was only that we expected her to wake up the next morning exactly like she always did.

Only she didn't.

Early the next morning, when I got up and headed outside, I could tell that something was terribly wrong. Mother and Father were in a panic. I quickly discovered that only seconds before Sophie had stopped breathing. I learned, too, that the midwife wanted to drape the sheet up over Sophie's head and pronounce her dead.[5]

Of course Mother wouldn't accept that Sophie was dead and none of the rest of us wanted to consider it either. Instead, Mother pushed the woman aside, ignored her fussing and complaining, and gathered us around Sophie's bed. She then grabbed Father's arm, and both of them dropped to their knees.

As best as we can recollect, Alvin, Hyrum, and I think that this is close to what was said and done:

"Joseph," Mother declared, doing her best to fight back her tears, "I know your brother, Jesse, doesn't think much on religion and praying. But I know you are a man of great faith. Our little Sophie has passed away, and if you'll exercise your faith with me, I feel certain we can bring her back."[6]

Mother really didn't give Father a chance to answer—although looking back on it, I don't think he even had any ready answer. In religious matters he usually let Mother guide the family, though he did preside over the table and took charge of religious meetings held in our home. In this, too, however, he allowed Mother to guide us, and so she said the prayer.

"Our Father who art in heaven," Mother began, her voice shaking and trembling, "we know we are poor mortal sinners, but we are also full of faith and praise for thee, and we love thee."

That wasn't the end of her prayer, but by then everyone in the room had grown still. We'd never heard Mother call all of us sinners before. I supposed her calling us all sinners was a new notion that we had to get used to. Accurate, perhaps, but definitely unexpected.

"Lord," Mother continued, "we pray thee to bless this house with health. And especially we pray for our dear little Sophronia. Thou knowest where her spirit has fled, and we pray thee to direct it to return to her body. She is needed in our home, and so we are here to pray her back."

I had my eyes tightly closed, but right then I opened one and took a peek at my sister's body. It hadn't moved, but I could see that both Alvin and Hyrum were also looking. It seems that they were as curious as I was.

Mother finished her prayer, Father turned and held her, and still not one of us moved. I didn't know what to do, so I just sat on the straight-backed chair in the corner and waited, certain that at any moment my sister would sit up and smile and be well.

She didn't exactly do that, but what happened next was about the same. Mother quietly arose, hankied up her eyes and nose, tucked her kerchief back in the front of her dress, and spoke.

"Children," she said, "the Lord has given me a witness that Sophie will live."

"He has given me the same," Father whispered.[7]

Mother looked at him, squeezed his arm, and then turned to us and spoke.

"What we need now is for the good Lord to answer our plea. He will, but each of us must pray hard and do our best to show him our faith. And don't any of you slack up until it happens."

Without saying more, Mother pulled the sheet back and lifted nine-year-old Sophie into her arms. She then began pacing, pressing Sophie to her breast, holding her eyes tightly, and praying.

I thought about looking over at Alvin and Hyrum, but decided that they would be praying like I ought to be. So I kept my eyes focused on the last little flame in the firebox and told the Lord over and over that it was up to him and that we were all waiting.

And then after only a couple of moments, Mother let out a peculiar squeal.

Naturally I jumped, but so did the rest of us. Most especially that midwife woman jumped, and I declare that her face turned white as a muslin sheet.

"Joseph," Mother cried, "come here! She's alive!"

It didn't take a second for us to crowd around Mother and Sophie. Sophie was sobbing and gasping for breath, her eyelids were fluttering, and her whole body seemed locked in a struggle to see which part could move the most.[8]

We were all relieved. But that midwife took one look at Sophie, let out a squeal of her own, and was gone. I don't recall that any of us ever saw her again.[9]

Mother hardly even noticed the woman's departure. She just sat on the edge of Sophie's bed, placed my sister's frail body once again on the feather tick, collapsed on the bed beside her, and began to cry.

The rest of us joined in, and before we knew it, Father was on his knees beside Mother, offering up one of the sweetest prayers I have ever heard in my life.

And that was Sophie's miracle.

Chapter VI

Sᴏᴘʜɪᴇ's ᴍɪʀᴀᴄʟᴇ ᴏᴄᴄᴜʀʀᴇᴅ only a few months before my illness. Naturally it was fresh in my mind, and so right off, when I heard the comments about removing my leg, I began silently but fervently praying for my own miracle.

My miracle came, but in a way that was different from Sophie's. Not less of a miracle, mind you, just one of a different nature.

"So there is dead tissue in our son's leg?" Mother inquired quietly.

"There is. In fact, there is a great deal of it in the bone as well as in the tissues."

"And it will always give him problems?"

"It will if he lives."

"And this is common?" Father asked incredulously.

"Not common, sir, but unfortunately frequent. Because of the dead bone, I call the disease necrosis.[1] Little has been written about it, however, and someone may have given it a different name, one that I have not yet found."

"And you believe that the only cure is amputation?"[2] Mother asked, her voice quivering.

Doctor Smith looked at her. "I didn't say that, ma'am.[3] I'm not even certain that there will be a cure. As I said, the boy is in a bad way."

"There will be a cure," Mother declared firmly. "Joseph will be fine."

"I hope so," Doctor Smith said, smiling gently. "And that being the case, amputation would be the most likely cure. Certainly amputation is what most of these men expected to effect here today. That is why we have so many of these young students with us. They will be needed to hold the boy down, for the pain will be severe."

"Oh, Mother, Father!" my sister Sophronia cried out from her forgotten corner, where she had been sitting quietly during the entire conversation. "Do not let them take off poor little Joseph's leg! Can't you pray and bring about a miracle like you did with me?"

Again my heart leaped with hope. It was not just I who felt the stirrings of a miracle. My dear sister Sophie felt them as well.

Father spun about in surprise. Mother put her hand on his arm and stopped him.

"I have prayed, my dear," she told my sister, "alone and with your father. That is why Doctor Smith is here. Now will you add your faith to ours?"

Sophronia nodded soberly and yet with great pride, for she knew of the hope that must have registered in my eyes.

"Good. Now, will you go find your brothers and ask them to pray with you?"

Again Sophronia nodded, and then she turned and was out the door and gone.

"Doctor Smith," Mother asked, turning back to the man in charge, "I feel that one more effort must be made to save young Joseph's leg. Isn't there another sort of procedure that can be tried, something you alone can do? I have heard that in similar operations you have cut portions of the bone away."[4]

I believe that Doctor Smith wanted another chance at saving my leg. However, he wanted all of us to know the dangers, for there were many; and most who had suffered as I had had eventually died of the infection.

At Mother's request, though, he smiled and agreed to try his procedure.

"Now, Mr. and Mrs. Smith," he cautioned, "you must be aware that this is not a proven technique. In fact, it is more in the nature of an experiment, though I have done it before with some success. With your son the damage is already extant, and he has been weakened to the point that he might not survive such a lengthy process. With amputation I would be finished in just moments, and though the shock would be great, there is a good chance that he would survive."[5]

"And this treatment will take a great deal longer?" Father asked.

"Much longer. Of course I can't see the extent of the damage inside the bone, but I might be probing and clipping off sections of bone for close to an hour. This is a great deal of time for a lad as young as he is to endure continual and tremendous trauma. Together you must all decide what I am to do."

Father and Mother looked at each other, and then they looked at me.

"Joseph," Father said, struggling to find the right words, "I feel that it would be safer for you to lose your leg."[6]

"I disagree," Mother stated flatly. "Joseph, my boy, it is your leg. What do you say?"

I gulped, for I feared the pain I knew was coming. Still, I wanted my leg, and so I entirely refused to consent to the amputation. "Doctor Smith," I said as bravely as I could, "I want you to try to save my leg."[7]

Doctor Smith nodded gravely, patted my shoulder, and then explained the procedure.

"The object of my surgery," he said, "is to remove the piece of dead bone, which has become a foreign body as it relates to the living tissue.

"The instruments I will use in this operation are a probe, knife, trephine or round saw, and one or more Heys saws. In addition, we have here several pair of strong forceps, and a pair of cutting forceps. As we begin, we shall lay all these instruments out on the table. We may not need all of them, but we must be prepared for the worst.[8]

"I know these instruments look awful," the doctor said, looking down at me. "But as awful as they look, I do not want you to be afraid of them, for we will be using them to try and save your life and your leg."

Doctor Smith then ordered that cords be brought into the room so that they could bind me down before cutting.[9]

"No, doctor," I quickly stated, "I will not be bound. I can bear the process better if I am not all tied down."

As I look back on it, I can hardly imagine that I said those things, or that I endured the surgery that was to come. I was such a little lad, and yet already I seemed to know what I did and did not want.

"Will you drink some brandy, then, Joseph?" Doctor Stone asked, anxiously trying to help.

I knew there would be no other way to take away the pain, and for a few seconds I remember giving it serious thought. But I also knew that I had once promised my mother that I never would drink liquor. I told Doctor Stone that, and so he tried once more, this time using a different approach.

"How about some wine, then? We need to give you something to take the edge off what will be happening to you."

"Sir," I answered, terrified and yet resolute. "I will not take alcohol into my mouth. Not on this day nor on any other."

Well, I'm not sure who was more surprised by my stand, my parents or those doctors. I could see that they were impressed though, and so I then told them exactly what it was that I would agree to do.

"I'll tell you what, doctor. If Mother will go out into the woods so that she cannot hear what is happening and if my Father will hold me throughout the operation, you can do whatever you want with my leg. That is, you can if you will promise not to cut it off."

Then before anyone, especially Mother, could protest, I turned to her and continued.

"Mother, please leave the room. I know you cannot bear to see me suffer. Father can stand it, but you have carried me so much and watched over me so long, you are almost worn out."

By this time I was crying hard, for I could not contain my tears. I know much of my anxieties were for my own pain, but I was concerned or my mother as well.

"Now, Mother," I concluded, trying to dry my eyes as I spoke, "promise me that you will not stay. The Lord will help me, and I shall get through it."

Reluctantly she agreed, and after hugging me and drying my tears, she set about getting everything ready for the operation.

Some elements of that day I recall with the greatest clarity, and others I hardly recollect at all.[10] For now, since my mother remembers some things better than I do, I will record her words:

> So after bringing a number of folded sheets to lay under his leg, I left him. . . . The surgeons began boring into the bone, first on one side of the affected part, then on the other, after which, they broke it loose with a pair of forceps or pincers: they then took away 3 large pieces of the Bone. When they broke off the first piece, Joseph screamed so loud with the pain of his leg, that I could not repress my desire of going to him. But as soon as I entered the room he cried out "Oh, Mother! Go back! Go back! I do not want you to come in. I will tough it if you will go."[11]

Mother immediately left the room again, and with all my heart I wished that I could leave with her. I was wracked with pain, and it went on and on so that I was certain that I would die before it ever ended.

And nowhere in all the earth was anyone who could take away the pain.

Chapter VII

Father," I cried, "help me! It hurts so. . . ."

My father, his heart aching because of the agony I was experiencing, his own eyes swimming with tears, desperately searched his mind for something to say.

"Joseph," he said, "be strong. You must be strong. You can do it. You come from a line of very strong people."

Through pain-wracked eyes I tried to see him. "Father, can you tell me a story about them?"

"I'll do that," he said quickly, obviously as anxious as I was to help me get my mind off the pain. "They've had trials themselves, terrible trials. But they are strong people, strong and determined, and they'd be pleased to see how well you're handling this."

"They would?"

"Most certainly. Your Grandfather Smith is named Asael, though folks call him Crooked-Neck Smith. He is very strong, and my mother, Mary, is strong, too. In fact, I have an Aunt Eunice who can take up a barrel of cider and drink out of the bung.[1] I think Mother must be almost as strong as that, and maybe even more so.

"When your grandfather was little," my father continued, "he burned his neck cords in some sort of fire. It must have pained him fierce, but he did little complaining, and it finally healed. Of course it caused him to have a slightly twisted neck, and that's why folks started calling him Crooked-Neck Smith.

"In fact, I hear tell that his neighbors consider his religious ideas to be every bit as crooked as his neck. Father figures that none of the churches on the earth are true, and that God's power is not here either. It may not be, son, but the power of faith certainly is. We saw your sister raised up, and to my way of thinking, that took some power. Another thing that Father says is that someone in his family will help to bring God's church back to the earth. I've often wondered who that might be."[2]

Concentrating on my father's words, I realized the pain did not seem so terrible as it had been. Forcing my mind to keep moving so that the pain of my operation would be shut out, I spoke.

"He seems mighty serious," I whispered.

"Sometimes. Of course he has his humorous side, too. I recollect a ditty he wrote when we lived in Topsfield. He sent it to a selectman pleading his tax assessment. Want to hear it?"

I tried to nod—don't think I did so—but Father told me the ditty anyway.

Three heffers two years old I own
One heffer calf that's poorly grown!
My land is acres eighty-two

Which search the record you'll find true;
And this is all I have in store;
I thank you if you'll tax no more.

Thinking about Grandfather Asael's property made me remember my other grandfather. Although I can't recall exactly all that I thought, these are things I know now, and so likely they would have been some of the things I considered that day.

Solomon Mack, Old Captain Mack he was called, was a lot of things. He was captain of his own ship, and he was a brave soldier. Once in the king's service he mustered two teams of oxen all the way to Fort Edward. Then he went back alone (except for one man who followed twenty rods behind him) in search of lost oxen. Suddenly, ahead of him four Indians came out of the woods, armed with tomahawks, scalping knives, and guns. Afraid it would be the end of him unless he could outwit them, my grandfather, unarmed, charged with his staff, shouting, "Rush on, brave boys! We'll have the devils!" When the Indians saw the man in the distance, they thought a troop was coming and fled.[3]

Although he was brave, he was also somewhat worldly and tried to acquire fine things and property. Mother says that he was always talking about money and land and such. Then a few years ago something happened to him which changed that. According to Mother, he got all crippled up with the rheumatism. She says he couldn't even get out of bed without the help of Grandmother Lydia.

I suppose his getting sick gave him time to read the Bible, because then and there, right in his bed, he got religion. Mother told me that one night he couldn't sleep, and then he heard voices and saw lights and other things, and he figured that he wasn't ready to die—at least not with his worldly sins still upon him.

I was way too young to think much about Grandfather Mack's change, but ever since I can recall he has been riding around sidesaddle because of his rheumatism, telling everyone he meets to repent. He also published a book on his beliefs,[4] and so he spends his days peddling his book and declaring his conversion to Jesus.

I'm happy that he is my grandfather. I just—

Suddenly my thoughts disappeared, and I was aware that I was screaming again. Something had snapped. Something had broken with a horrible noise, and I knew, I knew—

"Father," I cried out fearfully as I writhed in agony, "did they take off my leg? I felt it! I felt it! Oh, Father, please. . ."

"No, Joseph," Father answered reassuringly, "that was only another piece of bone. Now relax, boy. Just take it easy, and they will be finished soon."

"Oh, Father," I gasped, "I can't stand it! Don't let them hurt me anymore!"

I was twisting then, trying to pull my leg away from the saws and forceps that the doctors held. But I was small and weak, and the medical students held my legs down as if they were locked in vices.

"Easy, son," Doctor Smith soothed. "We've about got it all."

He talked on, but I didn't listen, couldn't listen. Instead, I looked up at my father, pleading that he would hold me more tightly, pleading with my eyes that he would somehow take away my pain.

I saw then the tears falling freely from Father's eyes, and as he held me close against him I felt his love. Then for some reason I was away again, not listening to Father's words but thinking about him and Mother, not in that room but somewhere else—somewhere that had no pain nor agony, but only happiness and peace.

Chapter VIII

Joseph," Father said, his voice sounding soft and far away, "your mother was born in Gilsum, just a few miles from here.[1] She was born on July 8, 1776, which was just four days after the Declaration of Independence was signed in Philadelphia. She came from a large family, just like ours; the way she talks, you'd think they all got along famously.

"When she was a young lady, your mother left home to live with her older brother, Stephen. She did that to try and escape the grief caused by the death of her sister Lovina.

"Stephen's home was in Vermont, in a town called Tunbridge. She lived there only a few months, but during that time she met a young man who caught her fancy. His name just happened to be the same as yours and mine."

Father smiled, and I would have also if I had been able to.

"I've always been amazed by that, Joseph. The first gentleman to take serious notice of her, and Mother falls head over heals in love with me. Of course I was taken by her, too, and even though she returned to her father's home in Gilsum, she and I kept in touch by letter."

Father paused and I waited for him to go on; when he didn't, I looked up. Right away I could tell that he was watching the doctors. That put my mind right back where I didn't want it, and I instantly started twisting about, trying to get away from the pain.

"Joseph, Joseph . . . ," Father whispered.

"Oh, Father, talk to me! Please keep talking!"

"Uh, well, let's see. I was born July 12, 1771, in Topsfield, Massachusetts, and I was part of the fifth generation of Smiths to live there.[2] I was the third child, and I always loved being around people. When I was growing up, I was happy that I was one of the oldest in a family of eleven children."

My father's voice droned on about his home and so on. But my mind was traveling again, thinking of things Father had done with me that I thought were great sport.

He frequently takes us on long rides in his carriage, and when he does, he tells us his memories of his own childhood. He always talks about his good times, and then in the same breath he has to tell us how much harder he had it as a boy than we do. For instance, he tells us about never owning a horse, having no pump for their well, and so on. At least he didn't have any farther to walk to the privy than we do, so he can't make a brag out of that. I only wish that—

"Father," I gasped as I twisted toward him, "take it away! Please, take this away from me! It hurts awful and I can't . . . I can't. . ."

"Joseph, I know it hurts. But tough it, boy. I did when I was younger, and I know that you can!"

"You did?" I gasped. "You had typhoid when you were younger?"

"No, but I did hurt my leg,[3] and it was mighty awful. Would you like to hear about it?"

I think I nodded, though I am not certain that I did more than look up at him.

"When I was twenty," he said, "my father decided to buy some uncleared land in Vermont. He sent your Uncle Jesse and I ahead of the family to clear the woods.

"We worked hard, working by day and hunting for food both early and late, doing our best to stay alive. But the land was good then, and seemed like a paradise to us. The winters were long and severe, the summers cool; and the country abounded in wildlife— deer, rabbits, grouse, ducks, and geese. Lakes and streams had excellent trout and other varieties of fish. Plums, cherries, grapes, and berries grew wild, and so did many healing herbs, including ginseng. Sugar maples were also prevalent.

"So life was good, but still, that new eighty-three acre farm cost a full one dollar per acre, and so we pretty much had to make a go of it, or Father would lose all he had.[4]

"First we cleared an acre for a home, and then we built it, a mighty rough little log cabin. We covered the entire cabin with the bark of elm trees so that our family could keep warm that first winter.

"With the cabin finished, Jesse went back for the family, leaving me alone to clear more land. Only a day or so later I injured my leg while swinging a big double-bitted axe.[5] As I recollect, it glanced off a tree, and I was in serious trouble.

"Patching my leg up as best I could, I sat alone in that cabin and considered what to do. Winter was coming on, and I didn't fancy sitting there alone with a bad leg and likely starving or freezing to death. Besides, I couldn't work, for I couldn't get up the strength to swing the axe.

"So I decided to leave and travel the 140 miles back home, where I could let my leg heal in comfort.

"What I didn't know was that my father had become so lonely for me that he had packed up the family and, with Jesse leading the way, had begun the long trek to where we had cleared the land.

"It was October, and a chill was already in the air. I walked and walked, or rather I hobbled and fell and crawled and hobbled again, and I came to realize that 140 miles is a monstrous long tour for a crippled-up man.[6]

"Day after day I forced myself to keep going, though the pain was so bad at times that I passed out. I didn't have much to eat either. About all I had to go on was nerve, but I reckon I have plenty of that, or at least your mother says I do. So I set a goal to reach a particular tree off down the road, placed one foot down in front of the other, and finally I got to that tree. Then I did it again with a rock or a fence or another tree and then another, and in that manner I just kept moving forward.

"And then, just three days away from our old home, I ran upon the family, who were on their way to where I was supposed to be waiting.

"I was mighty tuckered out, and my leg was so bad that I couldn't walk on it at all. But I didn't know any better, so I was still hobbling along on a makeshift crutch, bad leg, and all.

"Father and Mother did their best for me there in the road, which was a whole lot better than I'd been doing for myself. And then, I turned around and accompanied the family to their new home."

"It sounds like you were a mighty brave man," I ventured.

"No, son, nothing like that. I just didn't want to be left there in the road, and Father likely would have left me, he was that ornery."

"Like you?"

Father looked hard at me. "Exactly," he growled. "You tough this out, boy, or we'll move and leave you to walk after us as best you can."

Of course Father was only teasing, for he had no way of knowing how truly prophetic his threat would one day be.[7]

The next spring Father commenced clearing the land again, and he was working on that project when into his life walked my mother. He tells us that she wasn't near as pretty then as she is now, but he took her hand in marriage anyway. On the other hand, Mother says that Father was far and away the handsomest man she had ever met; but since she married him, his looks have gone downhill fast. Father says that's due to her cooking, and she agrees, saying that surely must be the reason why his belt size continues to increase. No doubt about it, my folks are a caution to listen to.

It's mighty funny what a fellow's mind does when he is in pain. I knew I was suffering, I knew that Doctor Smith and the others were cutting and boring and chipping away at my leg, and I could even feel where the blood was running down onto the sheets.

Still, as I thought of Father and his bad leg, I sort of forgot my own pain by imagining his.

Why, I hadn't had to walk anywhere, not since I had grown sick. What would I have done, I wondered, if I'd had to walk 100 miles or so in the cold weather with my bad leg? I didn't think I could do it, leastwise not so well as Father had done.

Chapter IX

Suddenly, I was screaming again. Something had happened in my leg, something else had broken, and pain was washing over me like a hot red fire. Besides that, my head was pounding, the room was spinning, there were lights flashing before my eyes, and no matter how I held onto my father, I knew I was about gone.

"Father," I groaned, "I can't. . . ."

"Easy, son. They just broke out the third piece of bone."[1]

"Joseph," Doctor Smith confirmed, "so far as I can see, we need not cut, nor drill, nor saw any more bone."

"You mean it's over?"

"No, not quite. But there will be no more bone cutting. We have only to—"

"Oh, no!" I cried, interrupting the doctor. "Please close it up! Please don't hurt me any more." I could say no more, and though Father did his best to comfort me, I would not be comforted. I had suffered forever, I would always be in pain, and nothing on earth would ever change that!

Why, I wondered, hadn't I let them take off my leg? That would have been so much less painful! It would have been over by now, the pain would have been gone, and I—

"I've got to tell them I have changed my mind," my brain screamed. "Maybe if I tell them, the operation can be done with, I can go to sleep, and when I wake up the pain will have gone away."

I could hear someone talking. Through the red and black wall of pain that filled my eyes and my mind I could hear someone speaking, calling me, "Joseph . . . Joseph . . . Joseph. . ."[2]

My mind was so weak after my surgery that even though I could hear Mother calling out to me, I hardly knew she was once again in the room. I knew Father was there, for he had held me during that whole ordeal and continued to do so for a long time thereafter.

Thinking back on it now, I realize that that day was the first time I had ever thought about how much Father loved me, and how much I loved him. I trusted him, too, in every way. I knew that he wouldn't let the doctors do anything they weren't supposed to do, and the comfort I felt in his large and powerful arms is beyond my power to describe.

I would say too that my feelings for Hyrum have also grown. I am thankful that he held me and took care of me, especially when Alvin was working on the farm.

Actually I am indebted to both of my older brothers, because whenever the young people from Palmyra or Manchester tried to knock my crutches out from under me,[3] both Hyrum and Alvin would come to my rescue. It is a great blessing for me to have them as brothers.

Most important, though, I learned to trust God. I know that he could have healed me quickly, but he chose to heal me in his time for a purpose that is still unknown to me. Further, he allowed Father to find Doctor Smith, and he allowed Doctor Smith to know enough to save my leg. Thus in so many ways I am indebted to God for the miracle of my life and strong limb.

In the weeks and months that followed my surgery, fourteen separate pieces of bone worked their way out through the flesh and skin of my leg.[4] Purulent infection came out as well, and the leg continued to give me pain for months and months thereafter. In fact, during the course of our winter journey to Palmyra, where we now reside, I nearly had a serious setback.[5] But through the providence of the Lord, I was preserved.

My miracle did not come as suddenly as Sophie's, but I have little doubt that my recovery was a miracle. It was the kind of miracle that required our family to work at finding a solution. I will always be grateful that the Lord preserved my leg. But I am perhaps even more grateful that the Lord brought our family closer together. Through my struggle, as well as through Sophie's, the Lord has welded our family together in a way that would not have been possible outside this fire of affliction.

I pray that together we will always endure life's adversities with such faith and unity.

Appendix A

Found in Joseph Smith, Manuscript History, *Book A-1, located in the LDS Church Historian's Office, Salt Lake City, 131–32. It was dictated by Joseph Smith in 1838–1839. The complete account is also found in Reed C. Durham Jr., "Joseph Smith's Own Story of a Serious Childhood Illness," BYU Studies 10 (Summer 1973): 481–82.*

WHEN I WAS FIVE YEARS OLD OR THEREABOUTS I was attacked with the Typhus Fever, and at one time, during my sickness, my father dispaired of my life. The doctors broke the fever, after which it settled under my shoulder, and Dr. Parker called it a sprained shoulder and anointed it with bone ointment, and freely applied the hot shovel, when it proved to be a swelling under the arm which was opened, and discharged freely, after which the disease removed and descended into my left leg and ankle and terminated in a fever sore of the worst kind, and I endured the most acute suffering for a long time under the care of Drs. Smith, Stone and Perkins, of Hanover. At one time eleven Doctors came from

Dartmouth Medical College, at Hanover, new Hampshire, for the purpose of amputation, but, young as I was, I utterly refused to give my assent to the operation, but consented to their trying an experiment by removing a large portion of the bone from my left leg, which they did, and fourteen additional pieces of bone afterwards worked out before my leg healed, during which time I was reduced so very low that my mother could carry me with ease.

After I began to get about I went on crutches till I started for the State of New York where my father had gone for the purpose of preparing a place for the removal of his family, which he affected by sending a man after us by the name of Caleb Howard, who, after he had started on the journey with my mother and family spent the money he had received of my father by drinking and gambling, etc.—We fell in with a family by the name of Gates who were travelling west, and Howard drove me from the waggon and made me travel in my weak state through the snow 40 miles per day for several days, during which time I suffered the most excruciating weariness and pain, and all this that Mr. Howard might enjoy the society of two of Mr. Gates daughters which he took on the wagon where I should hive Rode, and thus he continued to do day after day through the journey and when my brothers remonstrated with Mr. Howard for his treatment to me, he would knock them down with the butt of his whip.—When we arrived at Utica, N. York Howard threw the goods out of the waggon into the street and attempted to run away with the Horses and waggon, but my mother seized the horses by the reign, and calling witnesses forbid his taking them away as they were her propirty. On our way from

Utica, I was left to ride on the last sleigh in the company (the Gates family were in sleighs) but when that came up I was knocked down by the driver, one of Gate's Sons, and left to wallow in my blood until a stranger came along, picked me up, and carried me to the Town of Palmyra.—Howard having spent all our funds My Mother was compelled to pay our landlords bills from Utica to Palmyra in bits of cloth, clothing, etc. the last payment being made with [drops?] taken from Sister Sophronia's [ears?], for that purpose, Although the snow was generally deep through the country during this Journey we performed the whole on wheels, except the first two days when we were accompanied by My Mother's mother, grandmother, Lydia Mack who was injured by the upsetting of the Sleigh, and not wishing to accompany her friends west, tarried by the way with her friends in Vermont, and we soon heard of her death suffering that she never recovered from the injury received by the overturn of the Sleigh.

Appendix B

Taken from Lucy Mack Smith account, original manuscript of Biographical Sketches of Joseph Smith the Prophet and His Progenitors for Many Generations.

I SHALL HERE BE UNDER the necessity of turning the subject to my 3 son Joseph who had so far recovered that he sat up when he one day sudenly screamed out with a severe pain in his shoulder and seemed in such e[x]treme distress that we were fearful that something dreadful was about to ensue and sent immediately for the Doctor who said he was of the opinion it was a sprain but the child said this could not be the case as he had not been hurt but that a sharp pain took him very suddenly ~~that he had not been hurt~~ and he knew cause for it. The physician insisted upon the truth of his first opinion and anointed ~~this the~~ shou[lder] with bone linament but the pain remmained as severe as ever for 2 weeks when the Doctor made a close examination and found that a very large fever sore had gathered between his breast and shoulder which when it

was lanced discharged a full quart ~~of~~ of Matter As soon as this sore
had discharged itself the pain left it ~~and shot~~ shooting like lightning as he said down his side into the marrow of his leg on the
same side. The boy was almost in total despair Oh Father said he
the pain is so severe how can I bear it His leg immediately began to
swell and he continued in the most excrutiating pain for 2 weeks
longer during this time I carried him in my arms continually
soothing him and doing all that my utmost ingenuity could sug-
gest ~~untill~~ to ease his sufferrings until nature was exhausted and I
was taken severly ill myself Then Hyrum who has always been
remarkable for ~~the~~ tenderness and sympathy desired that he might
take my place So accordingly Joseph was laid upon a low bed and
Hyrum sat beside him almost incessantly day and night grasping
the most painful part of the affected leg between his hands and by
pressing it closely in this maner the little sufferer was enabled the
better to bear the pain which otherwise seemed almost ready to
take his life At the end of 3 weeks he became so bad that we sent
again for the surgeon who, when he came made cut ~~his leg open~~
an incision of 8 inches on the front side of the leg between the
knee and ancle the distance of 3 inches and by continual dressing
his leg was somewhat releived untill the wound commenced healing when the pain became as violent as ever the surgeon again
renewed the wound by cutting to the bone the second time shortly
it commenced healing the second time and as the healing ~~prg~~ pro-
gressed the swelling rose at last a councill of surgeons was called it
was decided that there was no remedy but amputation When they
rode up I went to the door & invited them into another room

apart from the one where Joseph lay Now said I gentlemen (for there were 7 of them) what can you do to save my boys leg They answered we can do nothing we have cut it open to the bone 2 and find the bone so affected that it is incurable but this was like a thunderbolt to me. I appealed to the principle Surgeon present said I Doctor Stone can you not try once more by cutting round the bone and taking out the affected part there may be a part of the bone that is sound which will heal over and thus you may save the leg you will you must [not] take off the leg till you try once more ~~to save it~~ I will not consent to your entering his room till you promise this ~~This~~ they agreed to this after a short consultation; then we went to the invalid:—the Doctor said, my poor boy, we have come again. "Yes," said Joseph, "I see you have; but you have not come to take off my leg, have you sir?" No, said the surgeon, "it is your Mothers request, that we should make one ~~moore~~ more effort; and that is what we have now come for ~~now~~. My Husband, ~~look~~ who was constantly with the child seemed for a moment to contemplate my countenance; ~~a moment and~~ then turning his eyes upon his boy, at once all his sufferings, together with ~~and~~ my intense anxiety ~~seemed to~~ rushed upon my mind; & he burst into a flood of tears, and sobbed like a child. The surgeons ~~now~~ immediately ordered cords to be brought, ~~and~~ to bind ~~the patient~~ him fast to the bedstead; But ~~Joseph he subject child~~ objected, and When the doctor insisted that he must be ~~bound the~~ confined he said decidedly; "No, Doctor I will not be bound. I can ~~have endure~~ bear the process better ~~to be~~ unconfined. "Then," said Dr Stone, "will you

drink some brandy." "No," said the child, "not one drop." Then
said the Dr, "will you take some wine?" ~~for~~ You must take something, or you ~~never~~ can never endure the severe operation to
which you must be subjected. ~~Answered~~ "No, answered the ~~the~~
boy, I will not touch one particle of liquor; neither will I be tied
down: but I will tell you what I will do, I will have my Father sit on
the bed close by me; and then I will ~~bear~~ do ~~anything that~~ whatever is necessary to be done, in order to have the bone taken out.
But ~~mo~~ Mother, I want you to leave the room, I know that you
cannot ~~stand it~~ endure to see me suffer so. Father can bear it. But
you have carr[i]ed me so much, and watched over me so long, you
are almost worn out. Then ~~with his eyes swimming with tears~~
looking up into ~~laid he her~~ my face his eyes swiming with tears, he
said beseechingly; Now Mother, promise me you will not stay, will
you? The Lord will will help me ~~that to se~~ I shall get through with
it; so do ~~you~~ leave me, and go away off till they get through with it.
~~I consented to do so, and~~ To this I consented; so, after bringing a
number of folded sheets to ~~fold~~ lay under his leg, I left him, ~~went~~
going some ~~100~~ hundred yards from the house. The surgeons
began by boring into the bone, first on one side of the affected
part, then on the other after which, they broke it loose with a pair
of forceps or pincers: thus, they took away, 3 large pieces of the
bone. When they broke off the first piece, he screamed so loud
with the pain of his leg, that I could not repress my desire of going
to him but as soon as I entered the room he cried out Oh! Mother!
go back! go back! I do not want you to come in I will tough it if
you will go when the 3 fracture ~~was~~ was taken away I burst into the

room again and Oh! my God what a spectacle for a Mothers eye
the wound torn open to view My boy and the bed on which he
covered with the blood ~~which~~ that was still gushing from the
wound he was pale as a corpse and the big drops of sweat were
rolling down his face every feature of which depicted agony that
cannot be described I was forced from the room and detained till
they finished the opperation ~~and~~ after placing him upon a clean
bed with fresh clothing ~~he~~ clearing the room from every appearance of blood and any apparatus used in the extraction I was
permited to enter he now began to recover and when ~~go~~ he
was able to travel ~~his un~~ he went with his uncle Jesse Smith to
Salem for the benefit of his health hoping that the sea breezes
might help him in this we were not disapointed for he soon
became strong and healthy

Appendix C

Taken from LeRoy S. Wirthlin, "Nathan Smith (1762–1828) Surgical Consultant to Joseph Smith," BYU Studies 17 (Spring 1977): 319–37; originally published in J. S. Goodwin, "Lecture Notes taken at Dartmouth, delivered at Dartmouth Medical Theater 1812–1813," Dartmouth College Library; also Nathan Smith, "Observations on the Pathology and Treatment of Necrosis," Philadelphia Monthly Journal of Medicine and Surgery *(1827): 11–19, 66–75 (reprinted in* Nathan Smith, Medical and Surgical Memoirs *[Baltimore: William A. Francis, 1831], 97–121).*

NECROSIS (I.E., OSTEOMYELITIS)—This is a disease of considerable importance but surgical writers have said little about it. Bell in his treatise on ulcers says a little but it amounts to nothing. When matter is found within the bone, it should be punctured with a trephine (a small cylindrical saw) a little below the center so that the matter may be discharged. Sometimes it is punctured with a common perforating instrument with a point. When this is used, there should be a number of holes made, that it may discharge freely. . . . Nature begins to form new bone, which generally surrounds the decaying part, the dead bone is sometimes thrown out by the surgeon keeping the wound open. . . . The new formed bone is much larger than the original and confined [sic] both ends of the dead part within its walls. In this case, the dead bone should be cut with a trephine or Heys saw in the middle and extracted with a pair of common forceps. Sometimes the new bone may be cut with either of these instruments or a pair of strong cutting forceps. There is scarcely any case where the affected part may not be removed by the surgeon if he is skillful except in the bones of the hands and the feet. In the thigh or the leg the dead bone may be easily removed. Much perseverance is required in this disease. When the bone of any limb be removed, the limb should be kept in proper situation, that it may not be deformed. Some regard to time in this operation should be observed, for instance in the thigh, the operation should not be performed until new bone is formed in order that the limb may be kept in its proper length—the operation should not be deferred until the bone rots away, for in this case, the patient generally becomes a cripple the remainder of his day. By operating in the right time, a small piece being taken out it generally saves the loss of a large portion.

Respecting the operation, the cases which occur are so peculiar, and require such different methods, that nothing more than general directions can be given. The object, however, in every case is the same; that is to remove a piece of dead bone, which has become a foreign body as it relates to the living.

The instruments which may be wanted in this operation are a probe, knife, round saw, and one or more of Heys saws, several pair of strong forceps and a pair of cutting forceps. . . . When we undertake this operation, we should be provided with all the instruments named, as we cannot always foresee at the commencement of the operation, what instruments we shall need before it is finished.

When I first began to perform operations of this kind, I was under the apprehension lest so much bruising and handling of the soft parts, as is sometimes necessary, to dislodge a large sequestra unfavorably situated, might be followed with bad consequences, and some of these operations have been more laborious and tedious to myself and the patient, which I have ever performed, yet I have never known any untoward circumstances to follow such operations, of which I have performed a great many.

Appendix D

Nathan Smith to Professor Benjamin Sillman, 31 March 1813, taken from LeRoy S. Wirthlin, "Nathan Smith (1762–1828) Surgical Consultant to Joseph Smith," BYU Studies 17 (Spring 1977): 319–37; originally publish in Emily A. Smith, The Life and Letters of Nathan Smith, M.R., M.D. (New Haven: Yale University Press, 1914) 85-86.

DEAR SIR.... According to my promise to Dr. Cogswell, I intended to have visited you at New Haven last January, but before I was ready to set off on my journey, we were visited by a fatal epidemic and instances of sickness and mortality became so frequent that I was afraid to leave my family in such perilous times; and my fears were not groundless . . . four of my children have lately been affected by the prevailing epidemic, but by the Divine Goodness have nearly recovered. I believe this country has never before been visited by sickness which has carried off so great a number of adult persons in so short a time. In some towns of this vicinity which contain perhaps from 1000 to 1500 inhabitants they have buried over fifty persons since the first of last January. The disease has not yet much abated either in its violence or frequency of attack. We hear of new cases every day, and almost every day brings me an account of the death of some friend of aquaintance. How long this dreadful calamity will be suffered to afflict us, no one can tell; but we hope and pray that when the winter is over the disease will disappear. . . . The winter here has been long and severe. . . . Your obedient servant, Nathan Smith.

Notes

Chapter I

1. LeRoy S. Wirthlin, "Nathan Smith (1762–1828) Surgical Consultant to Joseph Smith" *BYU Studies* 17 (Spring 1977): 335; hereafter cited as *Nathan Smith*. There is no indication whether or not Doctor Nathan Smith charged the Smiths a fee. Eleven dollars, however, seems to have been his standard charge for such surgical procedures.

2. Lucy Mack Smith, *History of Joseph Smith by His Mother, Lucy Mack Smith* (Salt Lake City: Bookcraft, 1958), 46; hereafter cited as *History*. There is no data concerning the ownership of the Smith residence in Lebanon, New Hampshire. We know, however, that they were there approximately two years, that they had rented previously in Royalton, Sharon, Tunbridge, and again in Royalton, and that their intent while residing in all these communities was to better their circumstances until they might own another farm of their own.

3. Ibid., 56. Lucy remembers that she gave the doctor directions, though evidence suggests that he knew full well the procedure that needed to be followed. See also Wirthlin, *Nathan Smith*, 319–37.

4. LeRoy S. Wirthlin, "Joseph Smith's Boyhood Operation: An 1813 Surgical Success" *BYU Studies* 21 (Spring 1981): 138; hereafter cited as *Operation.* Nathan Smith seems always to have been called in later rather than earlier, and once expressed his frustration about it. "I have not been fortunate enough to be called in till matter is formed, and therefore have not had it in my power. . . ."

5. A fictitious character.

6. Donna Hill, *Joseph Smith: The First Mormon* (New York Doubleday, 1977) 18. See also Ivan J. Barrett, *Joseph Smith and the Restoration* (Provo, UT: Brigham Young University Press, 1973) 26.

Chapter II

1. There is some controversy over the year, but most scholars now agree that it was 1813.

2. Smith, *History,* 32. Alvin was born 11 February 1798 in Tunbridge, Vermont.

3. Ibid. Hyrum was born 9 February 1800 in Tunbridge, Vermont.

4. Ibid., 350. Sophronia was born 16 May 1803 in Tunbridge, Vermont.

5. Ibid., 351. Catherine was born 28 July 1812 in Lebanon, New Hampshire.

6. Ibid., 350. Samuel was born 13 March 1808 in Tunbridge, Vermont.

7. Ibid. Ephraim was born 13 March 1810.

8. Ibid. William was born 13 March 1811 in Royalton, Vermont.

Chapter III

1. A fictitious incident. It is unknown how, or if, the Smiths paid for the surgery on Joseph.

2. Wirthlin, *Nathan Smith,* 334.

3. Ibid., 332, fn. 48.

4. Wirthlin, *Operation*, 148–49. According to available information, it was approximately 18 weeks, 4½ months, from the time Joseph came down with typhoid fever to the time of his surgery. In that entire time the pain only occasionally eased.

5. Wirthlin, *Nathan Smith*, 327. In all the early documents the disease was referred to as typhus, though it has been correctly identified as typhoid fever. It is not likely that even Nathan Smith understood the difference clearly.

6. Ibid., 328. Correctly named, Joseph's complication was called acute hematogenous osteomyelitis.

7. Joseph Smith, *Manuscript History*, Book A-1 (Salt Lake City: LDS Church Historian's Office, 1838–1839), 131–32. Hereafter cited as *Manuscript*. For the complete account of this experience, see Appendix A, this volume. See also Smith, *History*, 54.

8. Smith, *History*, 54. See also Wirthlin, *Operation*, 148. "A quart of pus would have been a huge abscess in a seven-year-old boy."

9. Wirthlin, *Operation*, 137–38. He quotes from Nathan Smith, "Observations on the Pathology and Treatment of Necrosis," *Medical and Surgical Memoirs*, 97–121. The entire fictionalized dialogue in the story is based upon Nathan Smith's contemporary 19th century descriptions of the disease. See also Appendix C, this volume.

10. Ibid., 136. The practice of pulling the sequestrum (segments of dead bone) out of the flesh dated to the time of Hippocrates.

Chapter IV

1. Joseph called him Doctor Parker; but records reveal no Doctor Parker, only a Doctor Parkhurst.

2. Wirthlin, *Operation*, 132. The use of ether, the first anesthesia, was not demonstrated until 1846.

3. Wirthlin, *Nathan Smith*, 329, fn. 32.

4. Smith, *History,* 54–55.

5. Ibid.

6. Ibid., 55.

7. Ibid.

8. The identity of the surgeon is unknown. It may even have been the same man who attended Joseph previously.

9. Smith, *History,* 55.

10. Wirthlin, *Operation,* 148. Nathan Smith's contemporaries felt that if caught in time such drainage would halt the disease. However, he reported that in all cases he had treated, nothing he had done had been effective in halting the disease in less than fourteen days.

11. Smith, *History,* 56.

12. Smith, *Manuscript,* 131–32.

13. Wirthlin, *Operation,* 147.

14. Ibid.

15. Ibid.

16. Wirthlin, *Nathan Smith,* 337. "For members of The Church of Jesus Christ of Latter-day Saints it is important to realize that Joseph Smith received treatment that was generations ahead of current practice and was attended to, on at least one occasion, by the most highly trained and experienced physician in Northern New England who was also the only physician in the United States who aggressively and successfully operated for osteomyelitis and thereby prevented amputation. Thus Joseph received the best of care that was available for many years to come from a giant of a man who lived, taught, and practiced in Hanover, New Hampshire, only a few miles from Joseph's home." See also Wirthlin, *Operation,* 146. "Nathan Smith preceded workers in his understanding and treatment of osteomyelitis by one hundred years. Early drainage of infection, complete removal of sequestra, and the sim-

ple, patient treatment of a complex wound were the ingredients of his success."

17. Wirthlin, *Operation,* 149.

18. Smith, *History,* 56.

19. Ibid. See also Smith, *Manuscript,* 131–32.

20. Smith, *Manuscript,* 131–32.

Chapter V

1. Wirthlin, *Operation,* 135. "Even in this (20th) century in the immediate pre-antibiotic era, surgical cures were difficult to come by. The overall mortality was still high, and varied from 1.5 to 26 percent, with an average of 12 percent. Of the survivors, only 50 percent were cured by surgery. The experience to 1937 was summed up by one reviewer: 'The survey of the literature on acute hematogenous osteomylitis from January 1932 to June 1937, establishes clearly only one fact, and it is the only fact established clearly, namely, the disease has a poor prognosis.'" See also Wirthlin, *Nathan Smith,* 327, fn. 27. "Prior to 1910 typhoid fever was very prevalent in the United States. Estimates varied, but it was thought that 35,000 people died of the disease each year with an estimated 350,000 total number who recovered. Typhoid fever was the great killer of soldiers before World War I—in the Civil War there were 80,000 cases of typhoid fever among the Union Troops with a mortality rate of 37%. Typhoid fever is a febrile illness of several weeks duration caused by infection with *Salmonella tphosa.* The infecting bacteria are transferred from the intestinal tract (fecal discharge) of one person to the mouth of another. Great epidemics raged because of contaminated water, milk, and other food supplies. The epidemiology was discovered between 1850–1875."

2. Hill, 35.

3. Smith, *History,* 52.

4. Ibid.

5. Ibid.

6. This is fictional dialogue but is based upon what we know of the personalities of both Joseph and Lucy Smith.

7. Smith, *History,* 52.

8. Ibid., 53.

9. A fictional departure. Actually there is no mention of what happened to the woman, or women, as the case may have been.

Chapter VI

1. Wirthlin, *Operation,* 137.

2. Smith, *Manuscript,* 131.

3. Wirthlin, *Operation,* 149–50. The dialogue that follows is based upon Nathan Smith's own papers.

4. Smith, *History,* 56.

5. Smith, *Manuscript,* 131. Actually Nathan Smith brought fifteen years' experience with this "experiment" to Joseph's bedside. And although Nathan Smith had had very good results over that span of time and would continue to experience great success for many years to come, his work and results were not repeated until the early twentieth century. See Wirthlin, *Operation,* 153.

6. Ibid. According to Joseph, his father actually despaired of his son's life.

7. Ibid.

8. Wirthlin, *Nathan Smith,* 330–31.

9. Smith, *History,* 56–57. The dialogue that follows is based upon Lucy's history.

10. Smith, *Manuscript,* 131–32. See Appendix A, this volume.

11. Wirthlin, *Operation,* 152. This is a quote from Lucy Mack Smith's preliminary manuscript, "History of Joseph Smith," and is slightly different from her published account. See Smith, *History,* 57–58.

Chapter VII

1. Hill, 17–19.
2. Ibid., 24.
3. Ibid., 25–31.
4. Ibid., 25. This was ". . . a narrative of his life and published at his own expense, forty-eight pages tightly packed with information and at times quite vivid. However, it is hard to read because events are not always in sequence, and the printer did not trouble to correct errors, which appear throughout. . . . The facts of Solomon Mack's life as he states them, his holdings of land and his military and maritime experiences, are verified by official records which reveal that his claims, rather than exaggerated, were in fact modest.

Chapter VIII

1. Ibid., 32–33.
2. Donald Q. Cannon, "Topsfield, Massachusetts: Ancestral Home of the Prophet Joseph Smith," *BYU Studies* 14 (Autumn 1973): 72.
3. Hill, 20–21.
4. Ibid., 21.
5. The actual nature of Asael Smith's injury has not been verified.
6. Hill, 21.
7. Smith, *Manuscript,* 131–32. Though this dialogue is fictitious, Joseph was in fact forced to hobble on crutches much of the distance from Vermont to Palmyra, New York. See Appendix A, this volume, for the full account.

Chapter IX

1. Smith, *History*, 58.

2. Ibid. Lucy Mack Smith records her reaction to Joseph's screams:

"When the third piece was taken away, I burst into the room again—and oh, my God! What a spectacle for a mother's eye! The wound torn open, the blood still gushing from it, and the bed literally covered with blood. Joseph was pale as a corpse, and large drops of sweat were rolling down his face, whilst upon every feature was depicted the utmost agony!

"I was immediately forced from the room and detained until the operation was completed; but when the act was accomplished, Joseph put upon a clean bed, the room cleared of every appearance of blood, and the instruments which were used in the operation removed, I was permitted again to enter."

3. Hill, 36. Hill reports that Joseph used crutches for about three years and limped for the remainder of his life. See also Wirthlin, *Operation*, 153, fn. 65, which says, in part: "In 1928, the remains of Joseph, Hyrum and Emma Smith were transferred to their present gravesite. In the process of the transfer, some of the boney structures were described but no particular mention of the bones of the leg was made. A photograph of the three coffins with their contents was taken at a distance. I was allowed to study this photograph but because of the distance and the partial drapings with silk, I could not make conclusions regarding the presence or absence of changes consistent with healed osteomyelitis."

4. Smith, *Manuscript*, 131.

5. Ibid.